Peter's Christmas Eve Adventure

Story by Betty Organ
Illustrated by Shawn Martin

Tuckamore Books
a Creative Publishers imprint

St. John's, Newfoundland and Labrador
2010

We gratefully acknowledge the financial support of the Canada Council for the Arts,
the Government of Canada through the Canada Book Fund (CBF),
and the Government of Newfoundland and Labrador through the Department of Tourism, Culture and
Recreation for our publishing program.

Illustrations and book design © 2010, Shawn Martin

Printed on acid-free paper

Published by
TUCKAMORE BOOKS
an imprint of CREATIVE BOOK PUBLISHING
a Transcontinental Inc. associated company
P.O. Box 8660, Station A
St. John's, Newfoundland and Labrador A1B 3T7

Printed in Canada by:
Transcontinental Inc.

First Printing October 2010
Second Printing December 2010

Library and Archives Canada Cataloguing in Publication

Organ, Betty, 1970-
 Peter's Christmas eve adventure / Betty Organ & Shawn
Martin.

ISBN 978-1-897174-68-5

I. Martin, Shawn, 1969- II. Title.

PS8629.R48P48 2010   jC813'.6   C2010-904990-X

Mixed Sources
Product group from well-managed
forests, controlled sources and
recycled wood or fiber
www.fsc.org Cert no. SW-COC-000952
FSC © 1996 Forest Stewardship Council

- Betty Organ -
For my step-grandson
Peter Donald Blackmore-Squires

- Shawn Martin -
For my daughters
Hayley, Gemma, Tasha, Cyan & Kayla (Not pictured)

On the day before Christmas in a Newfoundland town,

Peter played with his friends as the snow fluttered down.

There was joy and much laughter, they whooped and they cheered.

It was Santa's big night with his team of reindeer.

The grown-ups were stringing bright lights on the eaves.

Dads wrapped up the gifts, while the Moms trimmed the trees.

Then night fell upon them, and winds turned to roars.

Young Peter raced home to get safely indoors.

He smiled at his Mother, almost tripped on the cat.

He was chilled to the bone, so he jumped in the bath.

Now dressed in pajamas and snug as a bug,

he rocked in the chair with his hot chocolate mug.

He crawled into bed, and said with a yawn,

"This storm might stop Santa from sleighing 'til dawn."

Then just before daybreak Peter heard such a racket!

He jumped from his bed and pulled on his warm jacket.

He headed outside where it was easy to see the ruckus

was caused by some moose near the trees.

Peter moved forward, but stopped in his tracks.

Half-buried in snow was a huge burlap sack!

"That's awfully strange," he thought, looking around.

Then Peter heard something, a strange groaning sound.

He blinked at the curious sight that he saw.

It was Santa Claus leaning against the shed wall!

"Well, hello!" called out Santa. "I need some help, please.

I'm covered in snow, and I'm starting to freeze!

"We hit a big snowstorm, and missed your rooftop.

I knew we were falling, but I just couldn't stop!"

"My sleigh runner's broken," said Santa, quite sad.

"My Christmas trip's ruined. I feel pretty bad."

"Well, Santa," said Peter, wiping snow from his eye.

"I'm not a sleigh expert, but I'll give it a try!"

Back to the house went the two of them quick.

Peter was sure he could help out St. Nick.

He sat Santa down by the stove to get heat,

with bakeapple pie for a Newfoundland treat!

Santa was worried. What an end to his day!

Young Peter dashed off to repair Santa's sleigh.

He trudged up the hill and then into the shed.

"I wonder," he thought, as he scratched at his head.

"Those old hockey sticks could be tied up with twine.

As Santa's new runners, I think they'll be fine."

He hurried on back to the broken-down sleigh.

"These sticks should be perfect. There must be a way!"

But the sticks were too thin and they broke with a CRACK!

Would Santa get stranded and never get back?

"Leaping live lobsters!" He yelled at the sky.

Peter was mad but he tried not to cry.

Back into the shed he ran, quick as an elf.

Then he spotted some oars on a long dusty shelf.

The reindeer watched Peter as he used the old twine.

He fastened the oars in near-record time.

Then he grabbed all the reins at the front of the sleigh,

And pulled really hard – but the oars both gave way!

Meanwhile, old Santa had finished his food and found

some dry clothes, which he thought looked quite good.

He came up the hill, grabbed his great burlap sack.

It was pulled altogether and flung over his back.

His clothes now made Peter break out in a smile.

He hadn't seen Papa's blue jeans in awhile!

The old flannel shirt all in red, blue and green,

and the big rubber boots made a colourful scene!

But Peter's huge grin now turned upside and down,

as he looked at the sleigh and the oars on the ground.

Then all of a sudden Peter ran straight away.

He had an idea that might save the day.

Those cross-country skis painted purple and white

might be the best thing to help Santa tonight.

He bound up the twine so the knots were secure.

These skis would make runners, young Peter was sure.

Then he pulled at the reins, it took all of his might,

and the sleigh moved ahead. What a glorious sight!

Santa stood grinning, then heaved up his sack.

The night was now passing, he had to get back.

They hitched up the team and they checked all the gear.

Old Santa looked happy, so did the reindeer!

"Peter," said Santa, "you're a brilliant young lad.

The best Santa's helper this Santa has had!

"Now it's time for St. Nick to say, 'Ho, Ho, Goodbye.'

My reindeer and I we must take to the sky."

He picked up the reins, thanking Peter again.

"You helped save my Christmas. You're truly a friend."

With a word to the reindeer, he flew from the Cove.

"Merry Christmas, young Peter, we are off to the Pole."

"Merry Christmas to you and to all a good night!"

shouted Peter as Santa flew clear out of sight.

So Peter crept back into bed without sound.

Would anyone know that St. Nick had been 'round?

But early next morning papa was surprised.

He'd found Santa's suit and he rubbed at his eyes.

"Was Santa our guest?" Peter's Mom shook her head.

"I really don't think so," was all that she said.

They looked at young Peter, whose eyes were still gleaming.

He wasn't quite sure if he simply was dreaming.

"I thought I heard something go crash in the night.

I must have been sleeping, it gave me a fright."

"Still, I think something happened,

'Cause that's Santa's clothes.

Was he really our guest?

Only Santa Claus knows."

Biographies

Betty Organ is originally from Bay D'Espoir, Newfoundland. She has worked with young children for several years as a student assistant, as well as through volunteer organizations. *Peter's Christmas Eve Adventure* is her second published work, and she has plans for many more. Betty currently resides in Portugal Cove-St. Philip's, and works as an administrator in St. John's.

Shawn Paul Martin received his certificate of Commercial Art from Cabot Institute of Applied Arts and Technologies in 1988. He then continued his Art education by attending Fine Arts School in Sir Wilfred Grenfell College, Corner Brook, where he graduated with a BFA (visual), in 1994. He is currently working as a Graphic Artist for *The Telegram*. Shawn lives in CBS, NL, with his wife, Natalia, and their five daughters, where he still continues his own artwork, as well as commissioned pieces.